THE GHOST OF PANNA MARIA

Written and Illustrated
By

Rita Kerr

EAKIN PRESS ◆ Fort Worth, Texas
www.EakinPress.com

Copyright © 1990
By Rita Kerr
Published By Eakin Press
An Imprint of Wild Horse Media Group
P.O. Box 331779
Fort Worth, Texas 76163
1-817-344-7036
www.EakinPress.com
ALL RIGHTS RESERVED
1 2 3 4 5 6 7 8 9
ISBN-10: 1-68179-124-2
ISBN-13: 978-1-68179-124-1

*This book is dedicated to
Theresa Bronder Dziuk and Emil Dziuk and
to the memory of their ancestors who came to Texas
to establish the first Polish settlement in America.*

Acknowledgments

The author wishes to thank the following people for their personal interviews in which they shared their stories and knowledge about Panna Maria: Eugenia Scholwinski, Emil and Theresa Dziuk of San Antonio; Mary Mika and Father Frank Kurzaj of Panna Maria. Special thanks goes to Clara Bass, librarian at the Institute of Texan Cultures, and to the children who enjoy reading about life in early Texas.

Contents

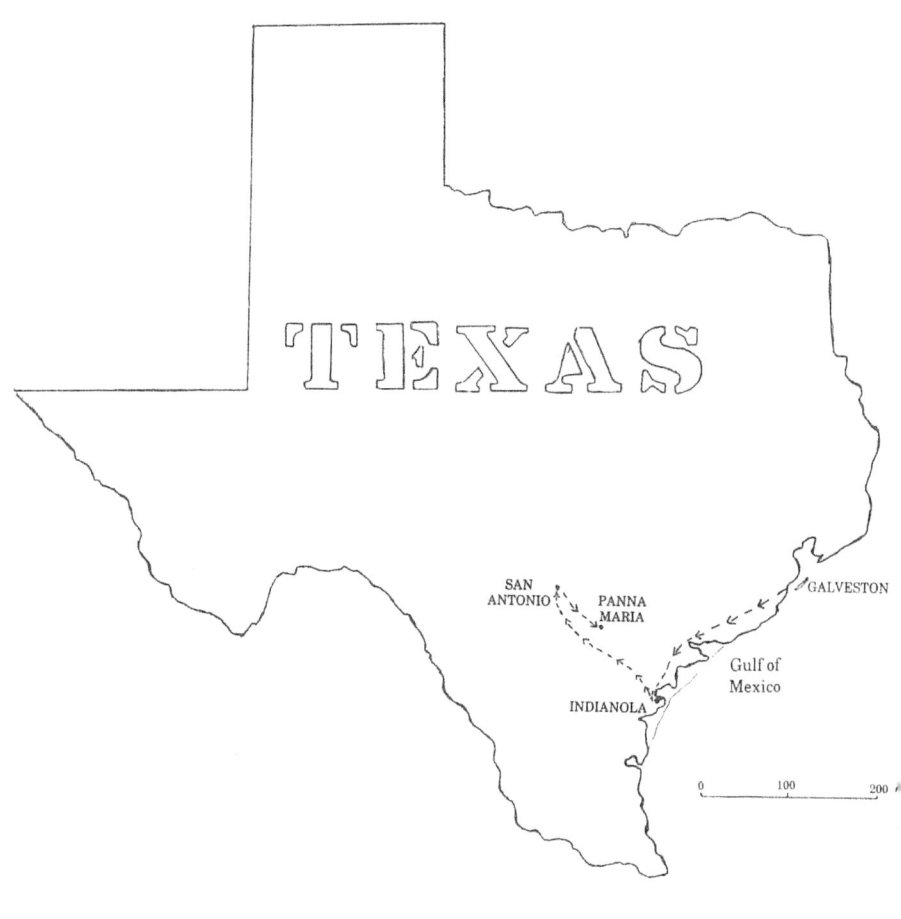

Preface

In the year 1854, under the leadership of Father Leopold Moczygemba, the first Polish settlement of America was founded at Panna Maria, Texas. After enduring a long, perilous voyage from Poland, the first Polish settlers faced many hardships in Texas. These included snakes, droughts, and Indians.

The historical facts in this book are documented. The ghost stories are based on folk tales and are, perhaps, fiction.

1

The Deadly Snake!

"Help! Jacob! Come quick!" screamed Anna Maria as she and her mother ran out of the house. Anna Maria's blond hair glistened like spun gold in the sunlight. Her two long braids swung from side to side as she waved her arms wildly, trying to get her brother's attention.

Jacob heard her screams. He clutched a pitchfork tightly with one hand and a hoe with the other as he raced toward her from the garden. From the fear in his twelve-year-old sister's voice, Jacob already knew what to expect.

"Where is it?" he demanded when he reached her side.

"In there — in the corner!" sobbed Anna Maria, wringing her hands excitedly. Her big, blue eyes were filled with fear.

"Be careful, son," Joanna Dziuk said nervously. "Oh, I do wish Thomas and Philip were home. If only those two dogs, Kos and Jos, were here, maybe they could help you. But your father took the dogs with him."

Her husband, Thomas, and their oldest son, Philip, had left the little town of Panna Maria early that morning. They had gone to Helena to trade their goats for a milk cow. Helena was a small village about five miles east of Panna Maria.

"I'll be careful," answered Jacob as he walked cautiously across the porch. "Now Mama, you and Anna Maria stay out here. Don't you come in."

He need not have worried. His mother and younger sister had no intention of going back into the house. Jacob laid the pitchfork down on the porch and grasped the hoe tightly with both hands. He stepped to the door and peered nervously inside, aware of the danger that waited for him there.

Like most of the houses in Panna Maria, theirs was built of stone and had a steep thatched roof. Jacob's father had built it much like their house back in Poland. The house had one door and few windows. There was a large fireplace at either side of the house, and a loft which extended the length of the roof. Jacob had shared one end of the loft with his older brother until Philip had gotten married. Now

2

he had it to himself. Hay was stored at the other end of the loft. There was a long porch at the front of the stone house.

After being in the bright sunlight, Jacob had trouble seeing as he entered the dark room. He stopped and looked carefully around. Suddenly, a slight movement in a corner of the room caught his eye. There, stretched out along the firewood in the woodbox, was a huge, long rattlesnake! It was the biggest rattlesnake that Jacob had ever seen!

How Jacob wished that he had a gun at that moment. But he knew that a gun cost a lot of money and his family could not afford one. They were fortunate to have food on the table and clothes on their backs. Life for them and the other Polish people living in Panna Maria was difficult.

Bravely gripping the hoe in his hands, the fourteen-year-old boy slowly advanced toward the woodbox and then stopped. He stood motionless. The snake slowly slithered across the woodbox. Its head was inches from the floor when it saw Jacob. Quickly the snake coiled its huge body and began to shake its rattles with a blood-chilling sound.

Jacob was so tense that he could scarcely breathe. As he stared into the snake's yellow eyes, he felt himself hypnotized and unable to move a muscle. The hoe fell from his nerveless hand and he stood helpless before the serpent. Just as the snake struck at him, Jacob managed to free himself from its spell and step back. His foot struck the hoe han-

3

*Raising the hoe, Jacob struck at the snake's head
with all of his might.*

dle and he fell to the floor. This saved him, for as he fell, the snake's fangs missed by only inches. The snake coiled again, preparing to strike at Jacob.

Frantically, Jacob tried to locate the hoe on the floor before the snake could attack him again. At last, he felt the hoe. Grabbing it by the handle, he scrambled to his feet, just as the snake lunged at him. It missed again, by only an inch! Raising the hoe, Jacob struck at the snake's head with all of his might. Again and again Jacob chopped at the deadly reptile with the sharp edge of the hoe. He felt as if he were beating only the air. Finally, after a number of powerful blows, the snake's head flew across the room and rolled to a stop under a chair near the fireplace. The body continued wriggling and flopping wildly across the floor. Jacob was grateful that the snake had missed striking him with its fangs.

Jacob shuddered as he watched the snake's headless body twist and squirm. He wiped his shirt sleeve across his damp forehead. His knees felt weak.

Jacob hoped that his family never learned how scared he had been. He had helped kill snakes before, but this was different. This time he had faced the danger alone — like a man. He doubted that his married brother, Philip, could have done better. But the job was not finished. Jacob knew that he had to get the snake out of the house.

He took a deep breath and picked up the hoe. Sliding the hoe's blade under the snake, he carefully

5

lifted the squirming body and carried it out of the door and into the yard away from the house. He then returned for the snake's head. Even in death those slanted eyes looked frightening.

Once the job was finished, Jacob gave a sigh of relief. He straightened his shoulders and smiled at his mother. "It is safe now, Matka. You and Anna Maria can go inside." Jacob and Anna Maria often called their mother Matka, the Polish word for mother.

His mother still had her hands folded. Jacob knew she had been praying for him. Their father had warned them time and time again to always carry a hoe or club and to watch where they stepped. There was always the danger of snakes or scorpions or spiders.

Anna Maria shivered. How dreadful that ugly creature looked. A cold chill ran up her spine. Those eyes seemed to be watching her. She hated snakes. They all did. Her father said that their fears were natural. There had been no rattlesnakes in Poland. They had never seen them until they came to Texas in 1854. Anna Maria wondered if Texas was the only place that had those awful creatures. She liked to think of animals being soft and cuddly like baby goats or puppies. Texas had many strange animals that were not soft and cuddly. There were armadillos and porcupines and skunks. Anna Maria did not like those either.

"Here comes Papa," Jacob shouted a short time

later. "And Matka, you and Anna Maria come and look. I think they traded the goats for two cows, not one!"

Joanna and her daughter hurried onto the porch. The dogs ran up to greet them as the men came into the yard. "Hush, Jos and Kos," Joanna scolded. With the dogs barking, it was difficult to hear. They all tried to talk at once as they looked at the two cows.

Anna Maria timidly rubbed each of their noses with her finger. "Oh, they look so gentle," she exclaimed, looking into the cows' soft, brown eyes. "What shall we call them, Papa? Anything so fine should have a name. We have named our other animals."

Her father chuckled softly. "What were you thinking of calling them, my child?"

"Well, this one could be Daisy. That white spot on her head looks like a flower," said Anna Maria. She stepped back to study the other cow. "And she could be Bossy or Flossy."

Jacob laughed at his sister. "We can't call her that. Our neighbor, John Gawlik, has two cows he calls Bossy and Flossy. How about a good Polish name like Babka?"

His mother looked shocked. "Babka? Grandmother? For a cow? Never."

"I have an idea," Philip said with a twinkle in his eyes. He looked at his little sister and said teasingly, "We can call one Anna and the other Maria."

"Well, this one could be Daisy. That white spot on her head looks like a flower," said Anna Maria.

The girl wrinkled her nose thoughtfully. She rocked on her heels looking from one cow to the other. "Anna? Maria? Yes, that is good." She folded her arms across her chest proudly. "Why don't we call them Anna and Maria?"

"No," her mother protested. "I would never know whether we were talking about you or the cows. Why not call them Daisy and Brownie? This one is brown and that one does have a spot on its head like a daisy."

Everyone agreed that the new cows would be named Daisy and Brownie. After that was settled, Joanna looked from her husband to her younger son. "Jacob, tell your father what happened."

They all looked at Jacob and waited silently for him to speak. No one moved as he began his story. Thomas rubbed his chin thoughtfully while his son explained how he had killed the snake. When Jacob paused to catch his breath, his father shook his head solemnly. "Is it still in the house?" he asked.

"No, Papa," Jacob replied, "I brought it out here. See?"

The two dogs barked nervously as they sniffed at the dead snake. Anna Maria noticed that no one wanted to get too close as they gathered around it. Philip stretched out his arms as if he were measuring the snake. He said, "Papa, I think that is the longest one we have ever killed, don't you?"

His father nodded. "That is a fact. I think it is the longest and biggest!"

Anna Maria's eyes shone brightly. She patted her brother's arm. "Isn't he brave, Papa? Aren't you proud of him?" She had no way of knowing how frightened Jacob had been.

"Yes," her father said slowly. "I am proud of him. When the weather was cold, we did not have to worry much about snakes. But now that the days are getting warm, we must watch for them. We cannot be too careful. You know what can happen to those who forget."

They nodded. They had heard terrible stories about people dying from snake bites. Although it was a warm day, Anna Maria shivered. The silence of the moment was broken by the ringing of the church bells.

"Oh," their mother exclaimed, "it is time for evening prayers. Philip, will you help your father tend to the animals while we go to church to give thanks for Jacob's safety and for the man who let us have these new cows? Come along, children."

The three started down the path. Anna Maria and her mother slipped kerchiefs from their apron pockets and tied them around their heads. They spoke to friends and neighbors who were also on their way to the church. Jacob hurried ahead to find his friends. He wanted to tell them of his adventures with the snake. The boys gathered around him to hear his story.

The Polish people of Panna Maria were deeply religious. Worship played a very important role in their lives. From infant baptism to the final rites at death, their lives centered around the church. Each Sunday since the church was completed in 1856, the Polish people from miles around had come to Panna Maria to worship. There was no other Polish church. Three different priests had served the church. The present one, Father Adolf, had been their priest for over a year. He was more than a minister. He had become their friend.

Anna Maria always felt that entering the dimly lighted church was like entering another world. She loved the hushed silence and elusive fragrance of the candles burning near the altar. It always gave her a feeling she could not explain. Anna Maria and her mother sat at one side of the church with the other women. The boys and men always sat on the opposite side.

Once the brief services were over, Anna Maria and the others walked out into the courtyard. The setting sun cast a rosy glow in the sky. She wondered how the countryside could look so peaceful and yet have so many hidden dangers.

2

The Trip to Texas

"Anna Maria," Joanna said one Friday afternoon, "now that you are home from school you must do your chores. The sour cream has been boiled. It is cool and ready to be poured. While it is drying, you can sweep around the house."

"Yes, Matka," Anna Maria said. She stretched a piece of cotton cloth over a bucket and slowly poured the pan of clabbered cream over it. The milky liquid slowly dripped through the holes in the cloth. The lumps of cottage cheese remained on top of the cloth. She carefully tied the four ends of the cloth together to form a sack. She then carried the sack outside and hung it over a branch on one of the bushes.

While the cottage cheese was drying, she got the broom and swept the hard-packed ground around the house. It was as smooth as glass. This area was kept free of grass in order to discourage snakes from coming near the house. While she worked, Anna Maria muttered softly to herself, "Thank goodness this week is almost over."

Each day while Anna Maria and her brother were in school, their mother was busy at home. Along with her usual chores of keeping house and cooking for her family, Joanna sometimes helped in the field. Each day of the week meant a special chore for her and the other women of Panna Maria.

Monday was wash day. On Tuesday they ironed. They churned milk to make butter and aired their bedding on Wednesday. Thursday was reserved for sewing and mending clothes. They made cottage cheese on Friday after they cleaned house and scrubbed floors. On Saturday, when Anna Maria was home from school, she helped her mother with the extra cooking and baking that was done to prepare food for Sunday. No one worked on Sunday. Sunday was their day of worship and rest.

"Papa said we had been invited to John Rzeppa's house after church on Sunday," Anna Maria said happily to herself.

John and his wife, Tecla, were one of the oldest couples in Panna Maria. They had been among the first Polish settlers who arrived in 1854. Since most of the people of Panna Maria had left relatives back in Poland, many thought of the elderly couple as their adopted parents or grandparents. They called him Grandfather and they called her Babka, the Polish word for grandmother.

Everyone loved John and Tecla. Since they lived near the church, they had many visitors on Sundays. The children looked forward to going to their house. Babka always had delicious cookies and she told the most wonderful stories. Her ghost tales could make their hair stand on end.

After church, on Sunday morning, Anna Maria and her family walked across the street to John and Tecla's house. They found that the couple already had visitors. Juliana Bronder and her children, Pauline and Pete, were there. Anna Maria and her mother went inside while Jacob stayed on the porch with his father and the other men.

"Come in, come in. Do find a seat," Babka exclaimed. "My, how you children are growing." Pauline and Anna Maria giggled. They were nearly the same age, but Anna Maria was the oldest. She was one of the three babies who had been born during the long journey between Galveston and Panna Maria when their families first arrived in Texas. Pauline had the honor of being the first child born and baptized in Panna Maria in February 1855. Pauline's brother, Pete, was ten years old.

"Please sit down. I will get the cookies," Babka said.

"No, let me get them, Babka," Anna Maria said

as she hurried to the kitchen. After everyone was served, she sat beside the others on the floor in front of the fireplace. The children listened politely while the women talked about the weather and their families.

During a lull in the conversation, little Pete spoke up. "Babka, will you please tell us a story?"

Babka smiled. She enjoyed telling stories. "Which one would you like to hear?"

"Tell us about coming to Texas on that ship," Pete said, grinning sheepishly. He had heard the story many times, but he wanted to hear it again. It was a story that never seemed to grow old.

Brushing the cookie crumbs from her long, gray skirt, Babka folded her hands in her lap as she leaned back in her rocking chair. With a faraway look in her eyes, she began to tell her story.

"We heard that Father Leopold Moczygemba was one of several Polish missionaries sent by the church to Texas in 1852. These men liked the land and climate of Texas. They were impressed with the freedom and opportunities that Texas offered to its settlers. Father Leopold thought that his family and friends back in Poland would like it too. He wrote letters telling them about this beautiful land. He suggested that they come to Texas.

"John and I heard that a number of younger couples were talking of joining Father Leopold. Most were plain, simple farmers just like us, and land was very important to all of us. We decided to join them.

15

But when the time came to leave, it was hard to say good-bye to our loved ones and friends. We knew that we might never see them again."

Babka paused in her story as she pushed a strand of gray hair away from her forehead. Then she continued.

"It was the end of October 1854 when we left our homes in Poland. There were one hundred families, consisting of about eight hundred men, women, and children going to Texas. Our family was with those who sailed on a ship named the *Weser*. A few of our group sailed on a smaller ship, the *Antoinette*. After everybody got aboard, we found ourselves crowded into a dark, windowless part of the ship. At night we had to sleep with two people on each small bunk. The bunks were covered with straw-filled mattresses. And the ship rocked from side to side as we tried to sleep. It was most unpleasant."

"Unpleasant?" Joanna exclaimed. "It was terrible! I was so seasick that I wanted to die. My husband had to take care of me and keep up with our two young sons. When Jacob and Philip weren't sick, they were into everything!" Anna Maria giggled at the thought.

Babka spoke again. "Oh, the ocean was rough indeed. Most of us had never been on a ship before. It was no wonder that many people got seasick. By the time that the trip was over, three of our group had died. We buried them at sea."

Pete asked, "How long did the trip take? What did you have to eat on the ship?"

"We were at sea for nine long weeks," she answered. "We ate salted pork and beef, peas, and sauerkraut. Tea and coffee and water were rationed. Considering the awful living conditions we had, it is a wonder that more people did not get sick. Isn't that true, Juliana?"

"Yes," Juliana replied. "We landed on the coast of Texas at Galveston on the first of December. I was happy to step onto dry land again."

Pete was eager to hear the rest of the story. "Then what happened?"

"Those who had money hired Mexican ox-carts to carry the things we had brought on the ship," Babka said. "How strange those carts looked to us. They had solid wooden wheels and were pulled by two yoke of oxen. The drivers wore broad-brimmed hats and striped blankets across their shoulders. They carried long whips to use on the oxen."

"Yes, and remember how the people at Galveston stared at us and our wooden shoes?" Juliana asked as she smiled. "They were shocked at the length of our skirts. They could see our ankles! The women in Texas wore skirts which touched the toes of their shoes. A few people laughed at the way we talked. I guess they had never heard anyone speak Polish before. Father Leopold told us that Panna Maria was the first permanent Polish settlement in America!"

"Well, English sounds strange to me. Did you laugh at them?" Pete asked.

"Of course not!" Pete's sister scolded. "It isn't polite to laugh at the way other people talk."

"She is right," Babka nodded thoughtfully. "You should never make fun of other people." Then returning to the story, she said, "We piled those carts high with our feather-beds, tools, and our cross. My husband made sure that we had his cross for the church that we would build. As we started out, we soon learned that the ox-carts were slow. They could travel no more than twelve to eighteen miles in a day. We walked beside the carts and carried what we could. We walked more than one hundred and fifty miles to get from Galveston to the town they called Indianola. It took us two long weeks! How disappointed we were to find that Father Leopold was not waiting for us. We were told that we should go on to San Antonio, where Father Leopold would meet us. So we started out again."

"But weren't you tired?" Anna Maria asked.

"Oh, so tired. We had set sail from Poland at the beginning of winter, so we were wearing our heavy woolen clothes. We quickly learned that the weather in Texas was not like that in Poland. We found that Texas had very unpredictable weather. One day it would be sunny and warm, and the next day would be wet and cold. There was usually a strong wind blowing while we were near the coast. When we stopped for the night, we had trouble finding enough

18

wood to keep the fire burning. After we turned inland, we found plenty of bushes, but there were few big trees."

Anna Maria's mother nodded. "And what trees there were grew in groves along the river banks. Sometimes the grass would be chest high."

"That is true." Babka's hand trembled as she pushed the strand of hair from her face once more. "Walking through that grassy wilderness was terrible. We were hungry. Some of our people were barefoot. We found it most difficult to walk over the rocky trail in our wooden shoes. I felt sorry for the poor little children. They were so frightened. Most of them clung to their mothers, crying from hunger and cold. Oh, we were all cold and homesick. Indians were a constant worry. Along the way we saw our first panthers and wildcats. We had never seen those animals before. Even the bushes and plants looked unfriendly."

Pete spoke up when Babka paused. "But why did you leave Poland in the first place?"

Babka looked at him with a wistful smile. "My boy, life in Poland had become hard too. There had been epidemics of cholera and other sicknesses. Our crops had been destroyed by insects and terrible droughts. We had come to Texas hoping to find a rich paradise and a healthier place to live. But our hopes slowly vanished as we walked along those long, lonely miles. We did not see a single person." She sighed deeply before adding, "We stopped only to bury our dead. Many died before we reached the end of our journey. And three little babies were born along the way." Everyone smiled at Anna Maria.

Pauline's mother nodded. "Remember how happy we were to find Father Leopold waiting for us in San Antonio? The people there could not understand our language and we could not understand theirs. It is a wonder that we ever found him, but we did."

"Yes," Joanna said, smiling in her direction, "I recall walking those last sixty miles from San Antonio to Panna Maria. How I carried a new baby and kept up with two small boys, I do not know. Thomas did what he could to help, but he was half-sick himself. We finally arrived here, under the big oak tree, on the evening of December 24, 1854. It was Christmas Eve."

"I remember it did not seem like Christmas Eve that first night when we had our midnight mass under the oak tree," Babka said quietly.

"That big tree out there?" Pete asked, pointing toward the church.

"Yes, the very same tree." She smiled. "We gave thanks and prayed for the strength to get through what lay ahead of us. The next day my John and some of the other men began digging holes in the ground to protect us from the cold. They covered the cavelike holes with grass to serve as the roofs. Those of our group who were too weary or too sick to work stayed under the oak trees. To make matters worse, it began to rain. It was a wonder that more of our people were not sick. We were all cold and wet. It was terrible."

She paused. "Texas was certainly not what we expected. We were all discouraged and homesick, but we had to have houses. At first we found nothing to use but mud and grass. For the roof we used the long grasses. Of course, the roof leaked when it rained."

"Why did you stay in Panna Maria if things were so bad?" Pauline demanded.

Babka shrugged her shoulders. "Some families did leave. At one time there were many more people living here in Panna Maria than there are today. Some moved northwest to San Antonio. Others went northeast to the village of Meyersville. Still others went on as far away as the settlement of Bandera. For those of us who stayed in Panna Maria, life was hard. There was little food and we had no way of getting any. We had no corn or wheat for bread. We might have starved if some of our American neighbors had not helped us. They heard of our problem and sent us twelve fine steers. Those kind people sent word for us to eat and be merry. They also sent us corn to make bread and seeds to plant. We were most grateful."

"Poor Father Leopold tried to help, but there was not much he could do," Juliana said. "I will never forget the day he called us together to encourage us. No one saw the rattlesnake crawling along a

*No one saw the rattlesnake crawling along a rafter
near the roof until it fell into the middle of the table.*

rafter near the roof until it fell into the middle of the table! I screamed and so did the others! It was just a wonder that the rattlesnake did not fall into our pot of soup!"

Everyone laughed at the thought.

"Yes," Anna Maria's mother said, shaking her head, "and then it didn't rain for fourteen months. The land was so dry and parched that even the wild grasses turned brown. The water in the river was not fit to drink."

"Yes, but by 1856 we did have a church in Panna Maria. Father Leopold said that it was the first Polish church in America!" Juliana smiled as she added, "Of course, it only had a dirt floor. There was no glass in the windows, and there were no seats or benches. And Panna Maria also had one stone house. It belonged to John Gawlik. Wasn't yours the second stone house, Grandmother?"

"Yes. And how happy we were to move in. After living in that mud house almost three years, this was like a palace. Today many of the houses in Panna Maria are made of stone like the ones we left behind in Poland," Babka sighed.

"Do you ever feel homesick for Poland, Babka?" asked Anna Maria.

"Yes, child, sometimes I do," answered Babka. "But Panna Maria is our home now — Panna Maria and Texas. And we have grown to love them. I am sure that all of the people who live in Panna Maria feel as I do. It has been twelve years since we arrived here, and many of the years have been very hard ones. But we have worked to earn this land and the right to live on it. And best of all, we live in a free country. Never forget that, Anna Maria."

Anna Maria knew in her heart that Babka had spoken a great truth.

For a few moments, the women and children in the room sat in silence. The children were thinking of the story that Babka had just told to them. The women were remembering the hardships that they had experienced in settling Panna Maria.

Finally, Pete broke the silence and asked politely, "Will you tell us the story about the big ghost dog, Babka? My father says that you know a good one."

"No, not now," Pete's mother said. "Babka is tired. Perhaps she will tell that story another day. It is getting late. We must go home now."

With many good-byes and fond farewells, Babka's guests walked together slowly down the path toward their homes. Anna Maria was disappointed that they had not heard the story about the ghost dog. But she thought to herself, *Since it is getting dark, perhaps it's best that Babka didn't tell the story or I might not sleep tonight.*

3

The Ghost Dog

Anna Maria and her family were invited back to the Rzeppas' house on the following Sunday. The Bronder family was there too. Again the men and boys sat on the porch while the women, along with the two girls and Pete, gathered inside the house. Anna Maria sat with Pauline and Pete on the hearth. They listened politely while the women chatted.

Everyone in Panna Maria was always eager for news from friends and relatives in Poland. Panna Maria had a post office, but the mail was slow. Poland was far across the Atlantic Ocean, thousands of miles from Texas. When a family received a letter, they were happy to share it with the others. Today Juliana Bronder had letters from her friends and loved ones back in Poland. She read aloud from the letters while everyone in the room listened intently. Pete waited quietly in the corner until his mother finished reading the letters. When she stopped, he turned to Babka. "Now," he pleaded, "will you please tell us the story about the ghost dog?"

She smiled as she looked into the boy's eager face. "My son, I must warn you. You may not sleep tonight if I tell that story."

"Aw, nothing keeps me awake," Pete declared bravely.

Pete's mother shrugged her shoulders helplessly when Babka looked in her direction. "He has talked of nothing else but that dog story all week. His father should never have mentioned it. Pete can't wait to hear it."

"Very well," Babka sighed. Leaning back in her rocker to collect her thoughts, the elderly woman folded her hands in her lap. The room was silent except for the creaking of the floor as she rocked slowly back and forth. Pete curled up at Babka's feet. She began her story.

"Most of the people of Panna Maria came from a part of Poland called Silesia. For as long as I can remember, the people of our village talked about a strange animal or creature that roamed around at night. Some said that it was a wolf. Others who had seen it said that it was a huge dog. No one was certain as to exactly what the creature was, but those who had seen it agreed that it always looked ghostly and terrible in the moonlight. And so, they called it the 'ghost dog.' We were always fearful of meeting it at night."

"Was it really big?" Pete asked.

"Yes, it was very big and fierce. Near our village there was a beautiful forest with many tall trees. Deep within the forest, some distance from our village, stood an old manor house. A rich and evil baron had once lived in that house. The older people of the village all agreed that he had been a cruel and terrible man. The villagers would not go near the manor house while the baron was alive. Now, the baron had been dead for many years and the house had remained deserted since his death. Some believed that the ghost dog had belonged to the evil baron and that the dog still guarded the manor house."

With eyes like saucers, Pete whispered excitedly, "Was the house haunted?"

"Some thought that it was. Strange things happened there. On dark nights, people who went near the house said that they could see glowing lights like fiery eyes moving about in the house. And they could hear strange noises coming from within."

Pete gulped. "What kind of noises?"

"None of them would say," Babka answered, rolling her eyes. "They were afraid to talk about what they had heard, and they refused to go near the house again."

Babka stopped to catch her breath. Complete silence filled the room. No one moved. Finally, with a deep sigh, she continued.

"One day a man from the village and his two sons went into the forest to hunt for deer. They sighted a large buck with beautiful antlers and began tracking him. As he moved through the trees and brush, the hunters were unable to get close enough to shoot. Yet they refused to give up the chase because he would provide a good amount of meat if they could shoot him. Deeper and deeper they moved into the forest, going farther away from their village with every step. When evening came, the deer was still too far ahead for a clear shot, but they fired their guns at him, each hoping for a lucky hit. The deer bounded away unharmed, and the hunters were left alone in the woods.

"Now, as they looked around, they realized that they had wandered too far and were lost. As darkness closed in around them, they began walking this way and that. But they could not find their way out of the woods. The night grew darker and darker and very little moonlight filtered down through the tall trees. They walked back and forth for hours, and it was very late when they came upon the old manor

*And then a horrible creature leaped out of the darkness
towards them!*

house. They moved across the clearing to the house and brushed the cobwebs away from one of the windows to look inside. They could not see anything. The windows were clouded with thick layers of dirt and grime. Suddenly, out of the darkness behind them, there came a terrifying sound."

Pete inched closer to Babka's chair. "Was it that awful sound?"

She slowly nodded her head. "Yes, that strange and awful sound. It was like a mournful howl that turned into a sobbing moan. The frightened man and his sons whirled around to face the thing that had crept upon them. And then a horrible creature leaped out of the darkness towards them! It looked like a huge dog, but it was not like any dog they had ever seen before. Its eyes blazed like fire and its teeth could tear a man to pieces. The creature's huge body seemed to change shape and waver in the moonlight, giving it a ghostly appearance."

"Was it a ghost?" Pete asked breathlessly.

"They did not wait to find out," answered Babka. "The boys and their father screamed and ran for their lives! The ghost dog was right behind them. They could feel its hot breath on their backs. The boys had trouble keeping up with their father as he dodged back and forth among the trees. By the time they found their way out of the forest, the boys could scarcely put one foot in front of the other.

"When they reached the safety of their house,

they bolted the windows and doors. They could hear it clawing at one door, and then another, trying to get in. The boys jumped into bed and pulled the covers over their heads. The man spent the rest of the night in a chair with his gun in his lap. When daylight finally came, the ghost dog had vanished."

The old woman paused. Pete shuddered. He let out a deep breath and asked, "Were they hurt?"

"No," Babka said, continuing her story. "All three of them had long marks on their arms. Their shirts were ripped and torn. People said that maybe they had torn their shirts on the branches of the trees. But that could not have been. Most of the trees in that forest were very tall."

"Babka," Anna Maria asked nervously, "is that story true?"

"I don't know." She was slow in answering. "Many of the people back home believed that it was true."

"What did the ghost dog want?" Pete asked nervously.

Babka rubbed her chin thoughtfully. "The older folks said it was wandering around looking for little children to frighten or harm. For years and years the children and most of the young people in our village were too afraid to go out alone at night. If they had to go out, they would repeat a verse that was supposed to be a charm to protect them from the creature."

"Verse? What kind of verse?" Pete demanded.

The old woman stared at the floor, trying to remember the words. "As I recall, it went like this,

When the night is dark, the ghost dog prowls;
He fills the air with his mournful howls.
His great eyes burn with a flaming light;
As he searches for children in the night.
So when darkness falls, stay in your homes;
And hide from the ghost dog as he roams."

When the verse was ended, Pete peered over his shoulder. "But that thing has never been seen here in Texas, has it?"

Before Babka could reply, Pete's mother gave a nervous laugh and said, "That's enough of ghost stories for now. You and the girls will not be able to sleep a wink tonight if we keep on like this. And I have to admit that the ghost dog frightens me too. Besides, it is getting dark outside and we must start home. We don't want to be out on a dark night after hearing a story like that."

As Pete started toward the door, Anna Maria heard him muttering to himself. It sounded as if the boy were saying, "When the night is dark, the ghost dog prowls . . ."

Later that night, hours after Anna Maria had gone to bed, she was awakened by a noise. It caused her to sit up in her bed, trembling. Something was clawing at the door and she could hear a low moaning noise. The door began to shake as the clawing became more violent and it looked as if the latch would break. Anna Maria's heart beat rapidly. She knew that the ghost dog was at the door. She knew that the creature was coming for her. At that moment, a wailing howl came from beyond the door and the terrified girl screamed, "Papa! Papa! The ghost dog is trying to get in!"

Her father jumped out of bed, grabbed his gun, and threw open the door. As he did so, Kos and Jos rushed into the room, whimpering. They were dripping wet and paused to shake the water off of themselves before seeking a warm, dry spot to spend the rest of the night.

"What is it, Anna Maria?" her brother whispered sleepily from the loft overhead.

Their father came back through the door at that moment and said to them, "It is nothing. Go back to sleep. It's raining hard outside and Kos and Jos were just trying to get inside where it is dry. Stop dreaming about ghost dogs, Anna Maria. It's only your imagination."

The next morning at the breakfast table her mother said, "Anna Maria, you must not believe all the stories that you hear."

"Yes, Matka," she said, lowering her big, blue eyes to stare at her empty plate.

"Jacob, bring in some wood for your mother. Then you two run along or you will be late for school."

When Anna Maria walked out the door, the two dogs wagged their tails, yawning sleepily. "Kos and

Jos," scolded Anna Maria, "you gave me an awful fright last night. You should be ashamed of yourselves." The dogs only wagged their tails faster. They seemed to be laughing at her. Then Anna Maria laughed with them. She had to admit that she felt a little foolish for believing the story about the ghost dog.

4

The Headless Ghost

One Sunday morning, Anna Maria's mother invited Father Adolf, Tecla and John Rzeppa, and Philip and his wife to have dinner at her house after church. There was plenty of chicken and dumplings and Polish honey cake for everyone. After they finished eating, the group moved out onto the porch, where it was cooler. Anna Maria and her sister-in-law sat at the corner of the porch with Jacob and Philip.

"All of you are my friends," the priest said, in a serious voice. "I feel that I must share something with you. Especially after what happened last night."

Thomas Dziuk spoke up. "What happened last night?"

"You have not heard?"

Everyone shook their heads. No one had heard a thing.

"Well, no doubt you will hear soon enough. I think you should hear it from me," the priest said.

"Hear what?" Philip asked.

"Well," Father Adolf answered, "early this morning Joseph Kyrish came to see me. He was most upset."

"Why? What was wrong?" Babka asked. "Was his wife sick?"

"I saw Lucia in church this morning. She looked fine." Anna Maria's mother answered. Lucia and Joseph Kyrish were their neighbors. However, Joanna looked concerned as she added, "But now that I think about it, Joseph did look pale."

"And well he should," the priest replied softly.

Again Thomas asked, "Why? What happened?"

Father Adolf began slowly. "Joseph told me that last night he went to see John Gawlik to discuss storing some hay in Gawlik's barn. On the way home, Joseph walked across the church grounds. There was a full moon last night, and he could see quite clearly. When Joseph came around the side of the church, he saw a tall figure in a black cloak going down the pathway." He paused. "At first Joseph thought that it was me and he started to call out. Then, just as he opened his mouth to speak, he

36

noticed something about the dark figure that sealed his lips. He knew that this figure could not be me." Again Father Adolf paused. He seemed to be choosing his words carefully.

"Joseph, shocked by what he had just seen, stood and watched as the figure glided slowly along in the moonlight toward the church. It turned the corner and went into the church."

"Who was it?" Philip asked.

"That was what Joseph asked me after he had told me his story. I had to tell him the truth. I had seen the figure too."

"Who do you think it was?" Philip asked again.

The priest shook his head. He did not speak.

Philip tried again. "About what time did this happen?"

"It was sometime after evening prayers. I was in my room. I had placed the lamp on the table by my bed and was sitting there studying. I suppose that I must have dozed, sitting there in my chair. Suddenly, I was awakened by a sudden rush of air through the window. The lamp flickered and went out. I walked to the window and looked out. There in the moonlight, I saw . . ." A long pause followed.

"Well?" Jacob exclaimed excitedly. "What did you see?"

"I saw a tall, ghostly figure dressed in a black cloak. As I watched, the figure moved slowly down the path and entered the church, just as Joseph said." Father Adolf solemnly bowed his head and stared at the floor. Everyone could see that he was nervous. He seemed to be having difficulty telling the story without alarming anyone.

"But who was it?" Jacob asked impatiently.

"I do not know. But . . ." The priest hesitated. He searched for words to tell them the rest of his story. "But . . . that is not the worst of it." He stopped once more.

"What do you mean? Go on. Tell us," Babka said encouragingly.

"My friends, you may not want to hear the rest," the priest said slowly, deliberately drawing out his words. Finally, he let the words tumble from his mouth. "The figure in the black cloak appeared to have no head nor hands!"

The women gasped in horror. Anna Maria saw her mother clutch the rosary pinned to her dress.

"No head or hands?" Jacob whispered loudly. "Are you sure?"

Thomas cast a sharp glance of reproval at his son.

After a brief silence, Father Adolf continued, "You see, last night was not the first time that I had seen the figure!"

The group blinked in bewilderment. "Not the first time? What do you mean?" Babka demanded.

The priest toyed with the tassle on the belt of his robe as he looked at them. "It was shortly after the new school was completed that I first saw it. That night, just as it did last night, the figure went along the pathway, turned the corner, and went into the church."

Jacob could hardly wait to ask, "Did you go inside the church to see what it was doing in there?"

"Yes, I was curious and so I followed it into the church."

"And what did you see?" Jacob asked, leaning forward.

"Nothing!"

In stunned silence everyone stared at the priest blankly. "Nothing?" Jacob muttered.

"Nothing! The church was empty except for the candles burning at the altar!"

"Oh!" Anna Maria whispered softly. She remembered that she and her mother had often lighted candles in memory of the dead.

A hushed silence fell upon the group. They had many unspoken questions. After Father Adolf's daring statement, each was wondering what it could mean.

Anna Maria's father broke the silence. He spoke softly as he stared into space. "You know, I never felt that we did the proper thing when we dug up those dead bodies and moved them from the old cemetery. That graveyard had been there since 1854, when we started Panna Maria. We had buried a number of our people there. Unfortunately, the cemetery was right on the very spot where people wanted to build the new school. Everyone said we had to move the dead to make room for the living. That bothered me.

Now, I wonder . . ." He did not finish. He thought it best not to say what was on his mind.

A cold chill ran up Anna Maria's spine. Some of the older boys at school had told stories one day about how the dead bodies were moved to the new cemetery. The stories were gruesome. For many nights after hearing them, she had nightmares about skeletons and pieces of bones. Anna Maria shivered at the thought.

The priest looked deeply concerned as he said, "Once people hear this story I fear they will say that we have a ghost in Panna Maria."

No one spoke. Anna Maria was silently thinking, *A ghost? In Panna Maria? That is impossible.* The idea made her shudder.

Later that night, Anna Maria lay in her bed and stared up at the hayloft. She thought about the tall, silent figure in the black cloak. Who could the ghost be? Why did it keep coming back? Could the ghost be one of the dead bodies from the old cemetery looking for its hands and its head?

Anna Maria drifted off to sleep, wondering what it could all mean. She rolled and tossed that night, dreaming about the headless figure.

As the days and weeks passed, the talk of ghosts slowly faded. The people of Panna Maria were too busy with fall planting and praying for rain to think much about a headless ghost. The cloaked figure had done no damage. Some people wondered if it had been a harmless prank. They talked about it less and less.

Late one afternoon in November, Anna Maria's mother looked up from her sewing. "Well, I declare," she said. "Philip left his coat here this morning when he stopped by. From the looks of that sky, it could rain. I would not be surprised if it turned cold before morning. If it did, your brother would need his coat. Would you and Jacob like to take it to him?"

"Yes, Matka," Anna Maria replied.

"Well, while you are getting your shawl I will call Jacob. I hear him chopping wood out back."

A short time later, Anna Maria and her brother hurried out the door. Their mother called after them, "You two hurry back. Don't you linger along the way."

Jacob threw his brother's coat over his shoulder as they headed down the path. They passed Joseph Kyrish's house and John Twohig's stone barn. That barn had served as their school until the new one had been built. They passed the Rzeppas' house, then turned north past the cemetery. Blas Dupnik's blacksmith shop, where Philip worked, stood nearby. Philip and his wife lived in the two-room house next to the Dupniks.

"Hey, Philip? Mary?" Jacob shouted, banging on their door. "You've got company!"

"Well, hello!" Philip said, opening the door. "What are you two doing here at this time of the evening?"

Jacob chuckled. "You went off and left your coat this morning. Mother told us to bring it. She thought you might need it by morning."

"She could be right. It does seem to be getting colder. Well, come on in and sit down." Both Mary and Philip were happy to have company. They insisted on serving Jacob and Anna Maria cookies and milk. With so many things to talk about, the time seemed to fly.

"Oh!" Anna Maria cried when she looked out the window. "It is dark. Mother told us to hurry back. She will be worried. It sounds like the wind is blowing too. Mother said it might rain. Jacob, we must go."

Anna Maria wrapped her shawl around her shoulders as they stepped onto the porch. A thick layer of clouds covered the sky. It had suddenly turned dark and was beginning to rain. "Listen to that wind. It sounds like hungry wolves," she cried.

Jacob started off, walking very fast, and Anna Maria had to run to keep up with her brother. When they passed John Gawlik's house, Jacob shouted, "Come on. Let's go this way. It is quicker."

Before she could protest, her brother had cut through the churchyard. Anna Maria cried, "Wait for me!"

Jacob did not hear her because of the wind. He shouted back over his shoulder, "Come on! I'll race you home." He was cold and did not wait for her reply.

Anna Maria watched her brother disappear in the gloomy night as she hurried after him through the churchyard. Her heart beat faster as she realized that she was now all alone. The sound of the chilling wind seemed strange and eerie to the frightened girl. She quickened her steps as she moved past the church. Oh, how she wished that she was safe at home!

Suddenly, she saw a shadow moving on the path ahead of her! It was some distance away and it was coming slowly toward her and the church. Anna Maria was filled with terror, for she saw that it was a tall, black-robed figure just like the one that Father Adolf had seen. She stopped and stood rooted to the spot in fear. Then, as the figure came closer, looming against the night sky, she could see that it had no head! She wanted to scream and to run. She opened her mouth, but no sound would come forth. Her legs and feet were rigid with fear and she could not move.

Closer and closer the tall figure came toward the terrified girl. Just as it was about to reach her, Anna Maria broke the spell that gripped her and screamed wildly. The figure stopped instantly and turned to her.

"My child, what are you doing out in the night?" asked Father Adolf as he threw back the robe from his head.

"Oh, Father Adolf," sobbed Anna Maria with

Then, as the figure came closer, looming against the night sky, she could see that it had no head!

tears of relief. "I thought that you were the headless ghost about to grab me."

"I am sorry, child, that I frightened you," said the priest as he comforted Anna Maria. "You see, I was walking back to the church and had pulled my robe up over my head because of the rain. I suppose that it did look as if I had no head. Come, my child. I will walk home with you. Why are you out alone on a night like this?"

"I was not alone," she sobbed. "Jacob ran off and left me."

They had not gone far when they met Jacob and his father, who had decided to go back and look for Anna Maria. When she saw her father, Anna Maria rushed into his outstretched arms.

"Oh, Papa," she cried. "I was so silly. I thought I saw the ghost. But," she was laughing and crying at the same time, "there was really nothing to be afraid about. It was only Father Adolf!"

"My child," the priest said softly, "you have learned a great lesson of life. We are often afraid of things that are not at all what they seem to be."

When they reached the house, Joanna took one look at Anna Maria and put her to bed. She was still shivering from the cold. Anna Maria could hear them talking to Jacob in the kitchen. Jacob was in serious trouble for running off and leaving her alone in the dark.

That night, Anna Maria dreamed of cloaks and ghosts and dreadful things.

5

The Polish Wedding

Spring came to Panna Maria after a cold winter. It brought new life to the trees and crops, and hope to the people. It also brought a wedding celebration. The first rays of the morning sun spread over the cornfields as Jacob and his father led their cows from the barn to the pasture. Back in the house, on this Wednesday morning, there was a flurry of activity. Anna Maria was humming a merry tune while she hurried to finish the dishes. The kitchen table was covered with loaves of golden brown bread. Joanna Dziuk lifted a pan from the fireplace and slid another one into its place on the hot coals.

"There, that is the last pan!" Joanna said, wiping the flour from her hands. "These loaves are cool enough now for me to put into the baskets."

The delicious aroma of fresh bread beckoned Jacob and his father into the warm, cozy kitchen as they returned to the house. "Um-m," Jacob exclaimed as he set the buckets of fresh milk on the shelf in the corner. "That smells good."

"Don't touch it. You will have to wait like everyone else," his mother scolded. "Did you two wash your hands before you came in?"

"Yes, and we combed our hair too," Jacob declared proudly. He eyed the bread hungrily as he asked, "May I help you?"

"You can stack these loaves in the basket, but do be careful how you stack them. I don't want any of them smashed. Lucia will need every loaf before this day is over." Joanna glanced up. "Anna Maria, have you finished the dishes? If so, you can run along. Just be sure you wash your face before you put on that dress. I don't want you to get it dirty. You may be needed to serve the guests. Now hurry. I told Lucia we would be there early."

"Yes, Matka," Anna Maria said, heading for her room. Her mother was lifting the hot pan from the coals when she returned. Anna Maria carefully placed a wreath of fresh flowers on her head and turned slowly around. "How do I look?"

Thomas Dziuk's eyes twinkled as he said, "You look just like your mother did when she was your age."

47

"Oh, Thomas," Joanna scolded. While smoothing the hem of Anna Maria's dress, she was silently thinking, *She is pretty with her dimpled cheeks and honey-colored hair. Someday she will be a beautiful woman. She reminds me of my own dear mother.* Joanna looked at her daughter more closely and said, "Your face looks clean and you've combed your hair. You look fine. Remember it is what is in your heart that counts, not how pretty you are on the outside."

"Yes, Matka," Anna Maria muttered softly. Her mother was right, but she longed to look pretty because today was special. They were going to a wedding! Rosalie Kyrish, the daughter of Joseph and Lucia, was getting married. The people of Panna Maria had talked of nothing else for days. A wedding was a big occasion. Friends and relatives of the bride and groom were coming from miles around. Many of the guests had begun arriving yesterday. Some had come on foot, and others rode in wagons or carts. Most brought gifts and baskets of food to help feed the crowd. Whatever they could afford, the guests had brought.

"I don't understand why Polish weddings are always on Tuesday or Wednesday. Why aren't they on Monday?" Jacob asked, putting the last loaf into his basket.

His father smiled. "Since we do not work on Sunday, the bride's family must have time to prepare the wedding feast. Joseph and Lucia have a big family and many friends."

"That is right," Joanna said. "This will be a big wedding. Lucia could not have done all the work by herself. She needed our help. Why, even with everybody helping, it still took us two days to get the turkeys and pigs ready to be stuffed. No doubt, Joseph will have them roasting by the time we get there. Babka and Juliana made the dumplings for the chickens while the other women made pies and cakes. It takes a lot of work to cook enough food for so many people. But we could not do much last week. The food would have spoiled since we have no way to keep it cool."

Thomas chuckled softly. "It is funny how we cannot have a wedding without food. They go together. Everyone will be expecting to eat three big meals today!"

"That is true," Joanna said, covering the baskets with clean cloths. "Well, I guess we are ready. Thomas, you and Jacob carry the baskets. Anna Maria, you carry the gift. But don't drop it."

"Oh, Matka, I would never do that!" She and her mother had spent many long hours sewing together the quilt that they were giving to Rosalie as a wedding gift. They had selected each quilt square with special care. This gift had to be pretty and practical. After all, Rosalie was Lucia's oldest daughter.

Joanna absent-mindedly patted her long hair, which was arranged in a bun on her neck. She reached for her shawl before she started out the door.

"Mama," Jacob laughed, pointing at her apron, "are you going to wear that?"

His mother threw up her hands in dismay. "Goodness! I forgot all about it. I don't want to wear an apron to a wedding." Everyone laughed.

The family started down the street. The dogs followed along behind them. "Kos, you and Jos go home. We don't need you at the church," Jacob scolded. With sad expressions on their faces, the two dogs turned back.

"Papa, why do the services start at ten o'clock?" Anna Maria asked.

Her father laughed. "Have you forgotten that wedding ceremonies are long? They are never over before noon. If they lasted any longer I would starve."

Jacob peered hungrily toward the basket he was carrying. "Me too."

"Oh, I love weddings," Anna Maria cried happily, clasping the gift to her heart.

"No, child, you like weddings, not love them," her mother said. "Love is something special. Your father and I love each other and we love you children. Love is eternal."

"Oh, I love you and Papa too. But I do think weddings are fun."

"Yes," her mother replied, "but never forget that marriage is a serious matter. Marriage for our people is 'until death do us part.' The bride and groom should know what they are doing. They must not be too young."

"How old were you and Papa when you got married?" Jacob asked.

His mother's eyes smiled happily as she looked up at her husband. "I was twenty and you were twenty-four, remember? My mother always said that a bride should be old enough to know her heart."

Other guests on their way to the wedding joined them before Anna Maria had time to ask her mother what she meant. Long before they reached the bride's home they could hear voices. They found that the yard was already crowded with guests. There were people everywhere. Some were gathered around a fire, watching the potatoes and sausages cooking over the open flames. Another group stood near another fire where the turkeys and stuffed pigs were roasting. The air was filled with excitement. Everyone was talking and laughing.

"Thomas, you and Jacob bring those baskets along to the kitchen. Anna Maria, you can put that gift over there on the table with the others. Then the three of you run along," Joanna said above the noise as she led the way to the kitchen.

Jacob found his friends near the dance platform, which had been built in the yard for this special occasion. Anna Maria located Pauline and the other girls standing outside the doorway of the house.

From that spot they had a good view of everything that was going on, in and around the house. The girls did not want to miss a thing.

"Sh — " someone whispered loudly, "Lucia and Joseph are ready to give the bride and groom their blessings."

The guests crowded around to watch the bride and groom kneel before Rosalie's parents. Receiving blessings from the bride's parents was a very important part of a Polish wedding.

After the blessings were given, the groom took his bride's hand and helped her to her feet.

"Come on, everybody," little Pete Bronder shouted excitedly. "Come on! They're going to the church!"

"We're going to the church! We're going to the church!" the other children chanted as they ran to join the wedding procession.

Two women remained behind to tend the fires and keep the roasting pigs and turkeys from burning. All of the other guests moved off toward the church. Everyone seemed to be admiring the bride.

"Isn't Rosalie beautiful in her wedding dress?" someone said.

"Yes, she is the perfect picture of a Polish bride," Babka agreed.

Rosalie was wearing her mother's wedding dress. Her ruffled petticoats peeked from beneath the brightly colored ankle-length skirt as it swished from side to side. Under her short, velvet vest Rosalie wore a white blouse trimmed with rows of lace. On her head she wore a crown of wildflowers woven together with colorful ribbons.

Anna Maria wondered why Polish women were not supposed to wear flowers in their hair after they got married. It was easy to tell the unmarried girls by their wreaths of brightly colored flowers. She thought her mother would look pretty wearing a halo of flowers too.

When they reached the church, everyone hurried inside to find a seat. The benches were quickly filled as the women squeezed together on one side of the aisle while the men were on the opposite side. The aisle and doorway were packed with guests who had to stand. All became silent as the services began.

Sunlight streamed through the open windows and made the solemn ceremony at the altar seem more beautiful. Anna Maria listened with rapt attention. She wanted to hear every word. She scarcely breathed as Father Adolf performed the marriage rites for the young couple in the quiet church. When the ceremony was over, everyone wanted to congratulate the bride and groom.

Jacob and the other teenage boys hurried for the door. Then the other guests began to file out of the church. They clustered together under the big oak tree, talking about the wedding.

Many of the women hurried back down the street to the Kyrish house. They had to be ready to serve coffee and sweet cakes when the hungry guests returned from the church. This would be their breakfast for the day. The wedding feast would not be served for another hour or two.

Soon everyone had gathered in the Kyrish yard again, and it began to buzz with activities. The older children played games while the smaller ones ran back and forth, getting in the way. Some of the men set up long tables in the yard for the food. Several of the women then decorated the tables.

Inside the house, the kitchen was crowded with women preparing the food. Some were stuffing the cabbage rolls. *Golabki* was a favorite with everyone. Another group was cooking potato pancakes. The children never got enough of those. The older folks always enjoyed the meat-filled dumplings called *pierogi,* which seemed to melt in their mouths.

Finally, all of the food was ready. A long line of women began carrying bowls and dishes of food to the tables. There were bowls filled with potatoes and some with cabbage rolls. There were huge plates of roast pig and sausage. The delicious odor of the food drew the guests to the tables.

There were not enough tables for all of the guests to sit together at one time, so it was necessary for them to eat in shifts. After the tables were loaded with food, the first shift sat down to eat. They were followed by the next shift. The large amounts of food quickly disappeared, for they were all hungry. After everyone had eaten, the men drifted to various parts of the yard to talk, and the children dashed away to play games. The women now cleared the tables and washed the dishes. Then they went to work to prepare the evening meal.

"Come on," someone shouted, "let's dance!"

The bride and groom took their place on the platform just as the fiddlers began to play. The dance floor was soon crowded. Young and old danced to the waltz and the polka. The sound of the music and their laughter filled the air.

Anna Maria stood at the edge of the platform and watched the happy couples whirl around. She was filled with excitement, and her foot tapped the ground, keeping time with the music. How she wished that someone would ask her to dance. She was so busy watching the dancers that she did not even see her brother until he spoke to her. "Anna Maria, would you like to dance?"

"Oh, yes, Jacob. I would love to," she cried excitedly. The platform shook to the "heel-toe-stomp-stomp-stomp" of the polka. Round and round they went. Anna Maria caught a glimpse of Philip and his wife whirling around the floor. Before the evening was over, she had danced with her two brothers and a number of the older boys. She liked the waltz, but the polka was her favorite dance. It was so fast and exciting.

The dancing continued until evening. Then food was again placed on the tables and the guests were served the evening meal. After the guests had eaten

The platform shook to the "heel-toe-stomp-stomp-stomp"
of the polka as round and round they danced.

and the tables had been cleared, the dancing began again.

"It's time for the 'Grand March'," someone shouted as the music started. The bride and groom led the dance. They could scarcely move for all the dancers. When the music stopped, two chairs were placed in the center of the floor.

"Come on, Rosalie," Philip shouted. "You and your husband sit down. Now, everybody, let's give Rosalie some money to buy herself a new hat!" It was difficult to hear the music above the clanging of the money and the laughter. Anna Maria wondered how that Polish custom ever got started. Few women in Panna Maria wore hats.

The laughter and noise slowly died as the fiddlers played their final song. The wedding celebration had come to an end, and the music faded away. The guests said their farewells and started home.

"Oh," sighed Anna Maria, as she looked up at the stars, "I wish this day would never end. It has been so beautiful."

"All weddings are beautiful, my child," her father chuckled softly. "Be patient. There will be another day just as wonderful."

Anna Maria whispered softly, "I hope so, Papa. I hope so."

6

The Phantom Rider

Two weeks passed and memories of the wedding celebration were beginning to fade. Life in Panna Maria had returned to normal once more.

One afternoon Jacob burst into the kitchen, bubbling with excitement. "Mama, Philip wants me to go with him to take a horse. May I go?"

"Philip wants you to take a horse where?" Joanna exclaimed, looking up from her ironing. "Where is your brother?"

"Here I am," Philip answered, walking into the dimly lighted room. He smiled at his mother. "My, it is hot in here!"

"Yes, I know." Joanna placed the heavy iron on

the fire to reheat while they were talking. She wiped her sleeve across her damp forehead. "But I have almost finished with the ironing. Now, what is this about Jacob going with you to take a horse?"

"Well, it is like this. Mr. Dupnik sold a horse to a man who lives on the other side of Helena on Butter Creek. Mr. Dupnik is not feeling well. He did not want to make the trip, so he asked me to go for him. Jacob could ride that man's horse and we could double up on my horse, Star, on the way back. It really would be helpful if Jacob went along. Otherwise, I will have to handle two horses by myself."

"Please, Mama," Jacob pleaded. "Philip needs me." It was not often that he had a chance to ride a horse. To ride the five miles to Helena was a rare treat that Jacob did not want to miss.

"Did you ask your father? He may need you."

Jacob nodded. "Papa said I could go. He told me to be sure you had plenty of wood before I left. Philip said he would help me chop more if you needed it."

Joanna's clear blue eyes met her oldest son's. "Did you tell your wife you were going? When will you be back?"

"We should be back before dark. It was Mary's idea for Jacob to go with me. I've got my gun. Also, Mr. Dupnik sent his in case there is trouble."

His mother frowned. "Trouble? What kind of trouble?"

"Oh, Mama," Philip laughed light-heartedly, "you know what I mean."

"Besides, I'm good with a gun if there is trouble," Jacob bragged, sticking out his chest proudly.

His brother gave him a warning glance, then said, "How about it? Can Jacob go?"

His mother sighed. "I guess so. But don't worry about chopping any more wood. There is enough here to last until morning. You two run along. Your supper will be waiting on the table when you get back."

"Thanks, Matka," Jacob said, bending to kiss her cheek as they headed for the door.

Joanna was surprised. Anna Maria often called her Matka, but the boys seldom did. And Jacob never kissed her on the cheek. He was too shy.

"You can ride that horse, Jacob, and I'll ride Star," Philip said, tossing him the reins. Jacob threw his leg over the horse and mounted it with ease.

Philip smiled to himself. He could see that his younger brother felt ten feet tall as they rode along. He understood Jacob's feelings. It was not often that they were alone together. They had never been to Helena without their father. And riding that handsome black horse would make any boy feel like a man!

They paused at the San Antonio River to water their horses, then rode on. They made good time and were in Helena before long. Philip looked around for the blacksmith shop. "Mr. Dupnik said to ask the smithy how to find the Spincer place. A good blacksmith would know everybody and everything about Helena," he said to Jacob.

They slid to the ground and tied their horses to a hitching rail. Then they walked into the smoke-filled shop.

The blacksmith smiled as they came in. "Howdy!"

"Hello," Philip replied. "I work for Blas Dupnik in Panna Maria. Do you know him?"

"Sure do. Dupnik's a fine fellow. What can I do for you?"

"We're looking for Joseph Spincer's place. Do you know where it is?"

The smithy grinned a toothless grin. "Sure, everybody knows Spincer. Just follow that road out there for about a mile. When you come to a creek — that's Butter Creek — just go on about half a mile. You will see his house up on the hill on the right. You'll know you're there by the dogs. Spincer's got five of the meanest dogs in Texas. But," the blacksmith winked one eye knowingly, "with all the mysterious things that have happened out there, I reckon those dogs have a reason to be mean. Just don't go into that yard until Spincer comes out, or you'll be sorry."

Philip nodded. "Thanks for your warning, and thanks for your help."

"Tell Dupnik hello for me," the blacksmith called over his shoulder as he turned back to his work.

Several people waved to Jacob and Philip as they rode through town. Jacob noticed the long shadows lying across the road. He looked at the sun and saw that it was near the horizon. He glanced over at his brother. "What do you suppose that smithy was talking about?"

Philip shrugged his shoulders. "Something mysterious, from the way that he said it."

They had no trouble finding Joseph Spincer's place after they crossed Butter Creek. They could hear his dogs barking long before they saw the house.

"From the sound of those animals, we had better not get any closer than this," Philip warned as they neared the house. "Hello. Is anybody home?"

No one answered. The five dogs barked wildly, but they made no attempt to leave the yard. "I hope those dogs stay up there. If they start this way, Philip, we will find out just how fast these horses can run!"

His brother laughed. "Say, maybe Mr. Spincer isn't home. He would have to be deaf not to hear all that racket. Why don't we both try calling him at the same time?"

"Hello! Hello!" they shouted.

A few minutes later a tall, gray-haired man with a shaggy beard walked from the shed near the house. He carried a big, double-barreled shotgun and wore a gun in his belt. "What do you want?" he yelled.

"Mr. Spincer?" Philip shouted back.

"That's right. And who are you?"

"I'm Philip Dzuik and this is my brother, Jacob. He's riding the horse that you bought from Mr. Dupnik over in Panna Maria."

The man shaded his eyes to peer at the horse. "Well, why didn't you say so in the first place? I would recognize that horse anywhere. Come on in."

"But," Jacob protested, "what about those dogs?"

"Down, dogs, down!" the old man scolded roughly. The dogs sat down. "Now they won't harm you as long as I'm here with my gun. But you better not try coming in when I'm not around. They'll get you!"

Mr. Spincer did not have to worry. Jacob had seen the dogs' teeth, and that was all the warning he needed.

"Now, you boys get down and come on in to visit a while. No need for you to rush off again so soon."

They tied their horses to the hitching post and turned toward the house. Jacob and his brother and the dogs eyed each other nervously. "Down, dogs, down! It's all right," Mr. Spincer said. But he walked between the dogs and the boys.

"Come on in the house and have a cup of coffee. Since my wife died, I don't have much company. The children are all married and have gone their way. Just me and the dogs and my horses live here now. Have a seat."

The boys sat down on nearby chairs. They watched Mr. Spincer take cups from the cupboard and fill them with thick, black coffee. It was the strongest coffee that Jacob had ever seen. It was thick as mud.

The man smiled ever so slightly as he handed them the cups. "I like my coffee strong and hot. Some nights I don't get much sleep."

"What do you mean?" Philip asked.

With a frown the older man replied, "I can see that you haven't heard about the unusual things that have happened along Butter Creek."

Jacob leaned forward curiously and asked, "What kind of things?"

"Well," the old man stroked his long beard thoughtfully, "there's a bush down by the creek that glows in the dark. You can see it sometimes from out there on the porch."

"What makes it glow?" Jacob questioned.

Mr. Spincer shrugged his shoulders. "Time and time again I have checked that spot. I can find no reason why that bush should glow, but it does. The dogs will not go anywhere near it." He paused, scratching his chin, and added, "And then, there's that tree."

"What tree?" Jacob asked.

"The one up on the hill. When the wind is right you can hear the clank of chains and the rattle of bones."

"Chains?" Jacob repeated softly.

"Yes. We started hearing them shortly after we moved here. My family was ready to leave, but someone suggested we do some digging around that tree. When we did, we found chains and old bones like from a human skeleton."

Jacob's mouth fell open. "Really?"

The man nodded. "At first I thought somebody was trying to frighten us off our land. Then we heard stories about prisoners or slaves being chained together and buried around here a long time ago. After we dug up those bones, we talked to our preacher. He came out and blessed that tree. Things have been pretty quiet around that tree since then, but I'm not taking any chances. I never leave the house without my guns. I don't suppose they would really do any good, though."

"Why not?" Jacob asked.

"There are some things you can't shoot. On stormy nights the lightning flashes and does a dance around that tree!"

Jacob glanced nervously out the window. "Philip, it is getting dark."

"Say, you're right. I didn't realize that it was so late. I'm sorry that we can't stay any longer. Now, Mr. Spincer, if you will sign this paper," Philip said, slipping the sheet from his pocket, "Mr. Dupnik will know that you got your horse."

"I wish you could stay longer. I have enjoyed your company," Mr. Spincer said, after signing his name. "Come back again when you can."

The boys watched the dogs cautiously as they walked past them toward the hitching post. Philip mounted Star and pulled his brother up on the horse behind him. "Good-bye, Mr. Spincer. Thanks for the coffee."

As they rode off, Mr. Spincer shouted, "Good-bye. Be careful when you cross the creek."

Now, why did he have to say that? Jacob wondered. They rode in silence. Each had his own thoughts. They reached Butter Creek and paused for a moment to let Star drink from the narrow stream of water. As they waited, Jacob asked his brother, "Do you believe all those things he said? Or is the poor man kind of touched in the head after living by himself with all those dogs?"

"I don't — " Philip began, but did not finish. "Sh-h . . . listen. Do you hear something?"

They could hear what sounded like a horse galloping toward them from up the creek bed. They did not move, but Philip's horse pawed at the ground nervously. The sound grew louder and louder. Suddenly, an icy cold wind swept by them as if death had passed their way. The boys shivered and their horse trembled with fear. They peered into the darkness, trying to glimpse the phantom rider. But the cold wind rushed on and they could see no one. The sound of the rider faded into the distance and vanished.

"Philip, what was that?" whispered Jacob as he

gripped his brother's waist tighter. "Let's get out of here before it comes back!"

"Giddie-up, Star, let's go!" Philip touched the horse with his heel. It was all that Star needed. She was off in a flash!

Jacob looked back over his shoulder and saw a shadowy horse and rider that seemed to be galloping after them. "Philip," he gasped, with his heart in his throat, "it's the phantom rider! He's after us!"

Philip cast one glance over his shoulder at the shadow that seemed to be gaining on them. Then he yelled, "Faster, Star, faster! Run as you have never run before!"

The gallant horse responded with a burst of speed, even though it could barely see its way through the darkness of night. For a few moments, they seemed to pull away from the phantom shape behind them. But the double weight of the two boys was more than Star could carry at a full gallop. Her pace began to slow, and as it did, the phantom rider gained on them.

Again, Jacob glanced back. He yelled in terror at what he saw. The phantom horse was almost even with them, and the phantom rider seemed to reach out to grab him.

Jacob shut his eyes and tightened his grip on Philip's waist. He expected to be snatched from Star's back at any second and carried off into the night. He could hardly swallow. His heart beat like a hammer.

He yelled in terror at what he saw, for the phantom horse was almost even with them and the phantom rider seemed to reach out to grab him.

Suddenly, Jacob sat upright. He listened intently and then opened his eyes and looked back. He saw nothing. He heard nothing. The phantom shape had vanished. Only the sound of their own running horse echoed in the night.

Philip, too, saw that the mysterious rider had vanished, and he slowed Star to a trot. However, they rode on for some distance before Philip paused to let Star rest.

"What was that?" asked Jacob, still recovering from his fright.

"I don't know, Jacob. I had my hands full with Star."

Jacob stammered nervously. "Would you believe me if I told you it had no face? Whatever that was, it looked like a big, black shadow — man, horse, and all. And suddenly — without a sound — it just vanished. It was a phantom rider in the night!"

"I believe you, Jacob, but I am not sure anyone else would. Maybe we had better keep this to ourselves when we get home. There are enough strange things happening without us scaring people."

His brother nodded. "I heard Mama tell Anna Maria not to believe everything that she heard. After this, I'm not going to believe everything that I see!"

7

Eternal Love

The days grew longer and hotter in Panna Maria as summer arrived. Jacob and his father had to get up earlier and spend more time in the field. One morning, at breakfast, Jacob exclaimed, "Um, those pancakes were wonderful! After a breakfast like that I will be able to do a good day's work." He pushed his chair back from the table, then stood up and stretched.

"That's good. We have plenty of work ahead of us, son," his father laughed. "Come along, now." The dogs followed behind them as they headed for the field.

"I must do the dishes before I go to school,"

Anna Maria muttered softly to herself. She did not notice her mother acting strangely until Joanna suddenly sank into a chair.

"Matka, are you all right?" Anna Maria asked in a worried voice. "You look so pale!"

"It is nothing," Joanna said. "This will pass."

Anna Maria knelt beside her mother's chair. "You should have told me that you weren't feeling well."

"I will be all right. Now, you run along, child, or you will be late. But hurry home from school. There is work to do."

"Matka," Anna Maria pleaded, "please let me stay home and help you today. You look sick."

"No, child. You know that we wanted both you and Jacob to finish school, but there is too much work for your father on the farm. He needs help. Jacob must stay home to help him, but you must finish your schooling." Joanna slowly got up from the chair. She did not want her daughter to suspect just how badly she was feeling. "Now run along."

"All right, Mama, but I would rather stay home and help you." Anna Maria headed for the door reluctantly. "Does Papa know that you aren't feeling well?"

"No, and don't you tell him! I don't need him in here fussing over me. Now run along, child."

"Yes, Matka."

Anna Maria was worried as she stepped into the yard. Her mother was hardly ever sick. Anna Maria

71

had never seen her so pale. She sighed, "It seems the work is never done. In the spring and fall Papa's either planting or plowing or pulling weeds. And Mama — poor Mama. No wonder she looks so pale. She's busy from dawn 'til dark. I wish I could stay home and help her." She thought of other girls she knew who had quit school in order to stay at home and help their mothers. Anna Maria knew that her parents would never let her do that.

She was so deep in her thoughts that she did not see her friend, Pauline, who fell into step beside her. "Good morning. Why are you so serious?"

"Oh, I was just thinking," Anna Maria replied with a half-hearted grin. Everyone said the two girls looked much alike with their big, blue eyes and peach-colored skin. Both had golden hair that hung to their waists.

"Can you come by my house this afternoon? We have some new baby puppies."

"Not today, Pauline. Mother is not feeling well. I must go right home after school."

With her lessons in reading, writing, and arithmetic, Anna Maria had little time to think about her mother. All of the studies were taught in Polish.

Hours later, when school was over, Anna Maria gathered her things and hurried home. When she came in sight of the house, she knew that something was wrong. On other days, smoke curled up from the chimney. It was a friendly sign that all was well.

Today there was no smoke. Anna Maria was afraid of what she might find.

"Matka, Matka?" she cried. The kitchen was empty. The fire was almost out. Her mother was not there. "Matka? Where are you?" Anna Maria called, running into her parents' room. Her mother was stretched out across the bed. Anna Maria sank to her knees and touched her mother's face. "Oh, Mama! You have fever! You are so hot!"

Joanna's eyelids fluttered open. "I had to rest for a little while, but I'll be all right. What time is it? Jacob and your father will be hungry. I must get up." But she could barely lift her head when she tried to rise. She fell back upon the bed.

"You stay there, Matka. I'll fix supper. But first I will get a wet cloth and bathe your face." Anna Maria ran to the kitchen for a wet cloth. She gently bathed her mother's face and hands. Joanna shivered.

"Are you cold, Matka?"

"A little," her mother said in a weak voice.

Anna Maria pulled the quilt up around her mother's shoulders and hurried back to add more wood to the fire. She looked around for something to cook. Jacob and her father would be hungry when they came in. Anna Maria put the pot of leftover stew and cold potatoes on the fire. While that was heating, she ran in to see about her mother. Joanna was sleeping.

"You have worked like a man today, son. I am

73

proud of you," Thomas was saying when they entered the kitchen. "Joanna?" he called. Then, surprised at seeing Anna Maria bending over the fire, he asked, "Where is your mother?"

Thomas Dziuk did not wait for an answer. He ran to the bedroom to see if Joanna was in there. Anna Maria followed him. He felt his wife's forehead and said in a worried voice, "Why, your mother is burning with fever. How long has she been like this?"

Anna Maria twisted her apron nervously. "She was like that when I came home from school. I think she's been having a chill. I covered her with that quilt. She has been sleeping for a little while."

"Well, we'll let her sleep. Perhaps she will feel better when she awakens. If supper is ready, let's sit down and eat. Jacob, would you mind milking the cows by yourself tonight? I want to stay near your mother."

"No, Papa, I don't mind."

The three ate in silence. They kept expecting Joanna to join them. When they finished, Thomas looked at his son. "I know you are tired. You worked hard today. But I want to be near your mother in case she needs me." He then went into the bedroom. Jacob patted his sister on the shoulder. Then he took the buckets off of a shelf and went out to milk the cows.

Anna Maria washed the dishes and fed the dogs. She wondered what else she and her brother should do. The house was very quiet. She jumped when her father called her name. "Anna Maria, bring your mother some water. She is thirsty."

"Is she better?" Anna Maria asked when she handed him the cup.

He shook his head. "You and Jacob go on to bed. There is nothing you can do. I will call you if there's any change. You run along now."

"But, Papa —"

"No, child. Get some sleep while you can. We do not know what tomorrow will bring. Your mother is very sick." His face was grave.

"Call me if you need me, Papa," Jacob said as he started up the ladder to the loft.

Anna Maria crawled into bed with her clothes on. She lay thinking about her mother until she drifted off to sleep. Suddenly, she was awakened by her father calling, "Anna Maria?"

"Yes, Papa," she answered, jumping out of bed.

"Do we have more quilts? Your mother is cold."

"She can have mine," she cried, grabbing the quilt from her bed. "I will put more wood on the fire, Papa. Maybe that will help. And I will make some coffee."

"What time is it?"

Anna Maria shook her head. "It must be nearly morning."

"After you build up the fire, then wake up your brother. I need him." Her father's face had never been more solemn.

"Can't I help?"

"I want Jacob to go for Doctor Zimmerman."

Anna Maria was stunned. They had never sent for the doctor before. None of their family had ever been that sick. What could it mean? She fanned the glowing embers to rekindle the fire. After Anna Maria was sure that the wood was burning, she climbed up to the loft. "Jacob, Jacob. Wake up!"

"Huh? What's the matter?" her brother asked, yawning sleepily.

"Come quick! Papa wants you to go for the doctor."

"Doctor? Is Mama worse?" Jacob was wide awake by then.

"I think so." Anna Maria felt the tears running down her cheeks. "Mama must be real sick. She looks so white and still."

"I'll be there as soon as I dress."

The coffee was boiling when Jacob came down. He tiptoed to his mother's room and whispered, "You wanted me, Papa?"

His father looked so tired and worried. "Your mother's fever is higher. She is having trouble breathing. I want you to go for Dr. Zimmerman."

Jacob stared down at his mother. Buried beneath the covers, she looked so small and frail. His sister was right, their mother was as white as a ghost. Jacob quietly retraced his steps. When he reached the porch, he burst into a run. The dogs opened their eyes to watch him race down the road.

Then, with a sigh, Jos and Kos went back to sleep. A short time later, Jacob returned with Dr. Zimmerman.

"Where is she?" the doctor demanded.

"She's in here," Thomas whispered from the doorway.

They both went into the room and closed the door. Anna Maria and Jacob stared at each other blankly. They were bewildered and frightened by their mother's condition.

"Well, we can't just stand here. I'll start breakfast. We have to eat," Anna Maria said.

Jacob could think of nothing else to do but light the lantern and head for the barn with the buckets. "I'll be back," he called back over his shoulder. The morning sky was filled with the first signs of dawn.

Anna Maria was setting the table when the doctor walked back into the kitchen with her father. The faces of both men were grim.

"You know, of course, that she is very sick, Thomas. With a fever like that, there isn't much I can do. I have no medicine strong enough to fight that kind of fever. It might be yellow fever or it could be something else. It is hard to tell."

Fear gripped Anna Maria's heart. Some of the Polish people had died of yellow fever. It was a dreadful disease.

"But can't we do something, Doctor?" pleaded Thomas.

"Just keep her warm. If you could break that

fever, there would be hope. See that she drinks plenty of water." Dr. Zimmerman looked down at Anna Maria. "Keep bathing your mother's face and hands. I'll have my wife bring you some broth. See that your mother takes it. If that is mush I smell," he glanced toward the pot cooking on the fire, "a little of that might do her good."

Anna Maria nodded.

"Oh, yes," the doctor added, "she should have no visitors. Your mother needs rest."

"But is there really nothing else we can do?" Thomas asked.

"You can pray. Pray and give her plenty of water. You know it might be good if you boiled the water. We can't be sure about how pure it is these days." Many of the wells had gone dry from lack of rain. People were forced to buy water for twenty-five cents a gallon. Some of the water they bought tasted bitter. "And you might heat two of those stones there on the hearth to put at her feet. Getting her real warm might help break that fever. I will be back later."

Jacob passed the doctor as he was leaving. Anna Maria insisted that her father eat breakfast with Jacob. While they ate, she went into the bedroom and bathed her mother's face and straightened the quilts. A short time later, her father brought the hot stones for Joanna.

Joanna opened her eyes and smiled at them weakly. Anna Maria knelt beside the bed and

Anna Maria knelt beside the bed and begged her mother,
"Please, Matka, take some water."

begged her mother, "Please, Matka, take some water."

Joanna shook her head and closed her eyes again. Anna Maria looked up at her father helplessly. It seemed there was nothing else they could do.

"Papa, you look so tired. You must get some rest. Why don't you stretch out on my bed? Jacob and I can watch her. We'll call you if there is any change."

Thomas reluctantly did as she suggested. When he put his head upon the pillow, he had never felt so weary. It was more than physical tiredness. There was an icy hand of fear gripping his heart. He felt powerless.

The morning passed slowly for Anna Maria. Mrs. Zimmerman, the doctor's wife, brought a pot of broth. She had also made chicken and dumplings for the family to eat. She did not stay long.

Each time their mother opened her eyes, the children insisted that she sip the water and take a little broth. Joanna drank very little.

It was early in the afternoon when the doctor returned. At the sound of his steps upon the porch, Thomas jumped out of bed. The two men went into the sick room together. Anna Maria busied herself by sweeping the kitchen again. Jacob took the ax and went outside. He said they might need more wood before the night was over.

Anna Maria was pacing the floor when her

father came out with the doctor. "Thomas," the doctor said, putting his hand on the worried husband's shoulder, "the next few hours are critical. Watch her closely."

"How could she be so sick so quickly, Doctor?"

The doctor sighed deeply. "You know, she probably has been having some fever for the past few days."

"But why didn't she tell me? She never said a word."

"Many people are like that. They won't admit that they are sick. Now, keep trying to give her water and broth. I will be back to see about her before dark. Of course, if you should need me before then just send Jacob." The doctor's voice fell to a gentle whisper as he said, "Thomas, it might be well if I sent for Father Adolf."

It was early evening when the priest arrived. He and Thomas went into the bedroom and closed the door. Anna Maria had many questions that she wanted to ask Father Adolf when he came out, but she was afraid to ask them. He put his arm around her and whispered softly, "I am sorry, my child. Be brave."

Sometime later Anna Maria heard a dreadful sob. She and Jacob ran to the bedroom. They saw their father kneeling beside their mother's bed. The children had never seen their father cry before. "Your mother's gone," he sobbed. Anna Maria and

Jacob sank to the floor and cried with him. They could not believe their mother was dead.

The next few hours were like a dream to Anna Maria. Jacob ran for his brother Philip and the doctor. The doctor came with his wife and Juliana Bronder. They went into the bedroom and closed the door. When they had finished, the family went in. Joanna was like a beautiful angel. She looked so peaceful and calm. Other people gathered to pray and to comfort the family, but Anna Maria could find no comfort. Her heart was broken, for her beloved Matka was gone. She sobbed and sobbed until she cried herself to sleep.

During the night, Philip and his friends made a simple, wooden coffin for Joanna. The next morning Blas Dupnik came with his wagon. Neighbors and friends walked behind the wagon to the cemetery. Anna Maria was too dazed to know what Father Adolf was saying during the burial service. She could only clasp her father's hand in hers.

When the services were over, everyone else walked away, leaving the family alone beside Joanna's grave. Anna Maria's world was shattered. She missed her mother more than she could bear. She knew that nothing would ever be the same again. Tears again flooded her eyes as she held her father's strong hand.

After a few minutes had passed, Thomas led Anna Maria and Jacob away from the cemetery with their hands in his. In silence, they began to walk along the path back toward their home, overwhelmed by grief.

Suddenly, a brightly colored little bird burst into song from a nearby tree. It seemed to be telling them that life must go on, in spite of sorrow. And then a ray of sunshine broke through the clouds overhead and bathed them in sunlight. To Anna Maria it was as if some power from above was reaching down to comfort and soothe her broken heart. She felt a calmness and peace returning to her troubled spirit. *Perhaps*, she thought, *it is Mama reaching down to tell me that I must take her place now, and become the woman of the house.*

Anna Maria's eyes followed the ray of sunshine up to the heavens, and she whispered softly to herself and to the sky, "Yes, Mama, I will try to take your place. I promise that I will. Please watch over me so that I won't make too many mistakes. You once told me that love is eternal. Now I understand what you meant. I love you, Matka."

A peaceful smile came to Anna Maria's face as she lowered her eyes toward Panna Maria and the future.

Bibliography

Books

Baker, Lindsay. *The Early History of Panna Maria, Texas.*
Lubbock: Texas Tech, 1975.
———. *The Polish Texans.* San Antonio: Institute of Texan
Cultures, 1982.
———. *The First Polish Americans' Silesian Settlements in
Texas.* College Station: Texas A&M University Press,
1979.
Boatright, Mody C., and J. Frank Dobie, general editor. *Back-
woods to Border.* Austin: Folk-Lore Society and University
Press in Dallas, Southern Methodist University, 1943.
Didear, Hedwig Krell. *A History of Karnes County and Old
Helena.* Austin: Jenkins Publishing Company, 1969.
Dworaczyk, Rev. Edward J. *The First Polish Colonies of Amer-
ica in Texas.* San Antonio: The Naylor Company, 1936.
Ebrom, Janet Dawson, and Richard Allan Sowa. *The Sowa
Family History: Six Generations of Polish Texans.* San An-
tonio: Sowa Book, 1981.
Przygoda, Rev. Jacek. *Texas Pioneers from Poland: A Study in
the Ethnic History.* Waco: Texian Press, 1971.
Rapstine, Carolyn, editor. *Roots of Faith: The Story of the Sa-
cred Heart Parish.* White Deer: Texas Sacred Heart Historical Committee, 1988.
Standish, Barbara Evans. *Texans, a Story of Texan Cultures
for Young People.* San Antonio: Institute of Texan Cultures, the University of Texas, 1988.
Starczewska, Maria. "The Historical Geography of the Oldest
Polish Settlement in the United States." *The Polish Review*
12 (Spring 1967), no. 2.

Miscellaneous

Carmack, George. "Panna Maria Honors Polish-born Pope." *San Antonio Express,* September 12, 1987.

Kilstofte, June. " 'With This Ring' Polish Wedding at St. Hedwig." *San Antonio Express Magazine,* April 9, 1950.

Institute of Texan Cultures. *Panna Maria: First Polish Colony in Texas.* Filmstrip series.

Merkner, Susan. "Polish Culture Moves Into Spotlight." *San Antonio Express,* July 7, 1989.

Census Records

Karnes County, Texas. 1860. Microfilm, Library of San Antonio Genealogical and Historical Society.

www.ingramcontent.com/pod-product-compliance
Lightning Source LLC
Chambersburg PA
CBHW070348130626
46556CB00007B/3077